Nelly
the
Monster-Sitter

Kes Gray

Illustrated b
Tony Ros

OXFORD

OXFORD
UNIVERSITY PRESS

Great Clarendon Street, Oxford, OX2 6DP,
United Kingdom

Oxford University Press is a department of the University of Oxford.
It furthers the University's objective of excellence in research, scholarship,
and education by publishing worldwide. Oxford is a registered trade mark of
Oxford University Press in the UK and in certain other countries

British Library Cataloguing in Publication Data
Data available

978-0-19-837723-8

1 3 5 7 9 10 8 6 4 2

Paper used in the production of this book is a natural, recyclable product
made from wood grown in sustainable forests. The manufacturing process
conforms to the environmental regulations of the country of origin.

Printed in China by Leo Paper Products Ltd.

Acknowledgements
Cover and inside illustrations by Tony Ross
Inside cover notes written by Sasha Morton

Contents

Chapter 1
Monster-sitting

"Are monsters real?" said Nelly, looking up from her comic.

"Yes," said her dad.

"Well, I've never seen one," said Nelly.

"That's because they never go out," said her dad.

"Why don't monsters ever go out?" asked Nelly.

"Because they can never get a babysitter," said her dad.

Nelly thought about what her dad had said. It certainly seemed to make sense. After all, her mum and dad never went out unless they could find a babysitter.

"I wouldn't mind being a monster-sitter," thought Nelly.

The next day, Nelly put an ad in the local newspaper.

It read: *MONSTER-SITTING After school and weekends. Call Nelly.*

MONSTER-SITTING
After school
and weekends.
Call Nelly

That evening, Nelly was eating her dinner when the phone rang.

"Hello," said Nelly in a bright and cheerful voice.

"Hullo," growled a monster in a deep, scary voice. "Can I speak to Nelly the monster-sitter please?"

"That's me!"
said Nelly.

"We were wondering if you might monster-sit for us?" growled the deep, scary voice. "My wife and I haven't been out since our lovely, furry baby was born. We'd so like to go to the cinema. Can you help?"

"Of course I can," said Nelly. "Where do you live?"

"Number 42," said the monster.

"I'll be there in an hour," said Nelly.

At seven o'clock, Nelly knocked on the door of Number 42.

The door opened with a creak and a big red eye looked out.

"Are you Nelly the monster-sitter?" asked the deep, scary voice.

"That's me!" said Nelly. "Can I come in?"

"Aren't you frightened?" asked the monster. "I'm pretty scary to look at."

"My dad says it doesn't matter how people look on the outside," said Nelly. "It's the way they are on the inside that counts."

"My name is Grit," said the monster. "And this is my wife, Blob." Nelly looked down the hallway. A blue, shaggy monster with green, dangly earrings was approaching.

"Pleased to meet you," said Nelly, shaking Blob's middle paw.

"Come and meet our daughter, Freeb," said Grit, leading Nelly into the living room.

Chapter 2
A Good Start

Freeb was doing a jigsaw on the carpet.

"She's very hairy, isn't she?" said Nelly.

"Thank you," said Blob proudly.
"We think she's got her dad's eye, too."

Nelly sat down with Freeb and began looking for some edge pieces.

"OK," said Nelly. "You go and have some fun. Please be back by 9.30."

The two monsters left Nelly with
Freeb and came back at nine o'clock
with a big tub of popcorn in their
paws.

"This is for you, Nelly," said Grit.

"The film was really good," smiled Blob. "We've had a lovely time."

"So have I," said Nelly, kissing Freeb on the forehead.

"If you want to go out again, just ring me," said Nelly, waving goodbye.

The next evening, the phone rang again.

"Hello," said Nelly.

"Hillooo," said a growly, snarly voice. "Are you Nelly the monster-sitter?"

"That's me!" said Nelly. "Where do you live?"

"Number 76," said the monster.

"I'll be round at 6.30," said Nelly.

At 6.30, Nelly rang the doorbell of Number 76.

The door opened slowly and two large, spiky heads peeped nervously round the door.

"Hello," said Nelly. "I'm Nelly the monster-sitter. Can I come in?"

Green, scaly fingers pulled the door open and Nelly stepped inside.

Chapter 3
Lump, Blotch and Bog

"I like your two heads," said Nelly with a smile.

"Really?" said the monster. "We thought you might be frightened."

"Two heads are better than one, my mum always says," smiled Nelly.

The green, scaly, two-headed monster took Nelly inside to meet his yellow, scaly, two-headed wife and pink, scaly, two-headed daughter.

"Her name is Lump," said the green, scaly monster. "She loves building with play bricks."

"I'll see what we can build together, then!" chuckled Nelly.

The two monsters left Nelly with Lump
and went to have some fun.

"Be back by 8.30," said Nelly.

At 8.15, the two monsters
returned with a big stick of pink
candyfloss in their hands.

"This is for you," said Lump's mum.
"We've been to the fair. We've had a super
time."

"I've had a super time too," said Nelly,
kissing Lump on both foreheads.

The next evening, Nelly's
phone rang again.

"Hello," said Nelly.

"Hellope," said a
sucking, thwucking
voice.

"Can you monster-sit for us, too,
please?" said the monster from
Number 93.

"I'd love to!" said Nelly. "I'll be round
at 7.15."

At 7.15 Nelly knocked on the door of Number 93. The door opened and a purple, rubbery head poked out.

"Are you Nelly the monster-sitter?" asked the monster with a suckery thwuck.

"That's me!" said Nelly. "Can I come in?"

The purple, rubbery monster
opened the door and Nelly
went inside to meet her purple,
thwuckery husband.

They had thwuckery, suckery twins.
"How can you tell the difference?"
asked Nelly.

"Blotch has a tiny, orange birth mark behind her fourth ear," said the monster mum lovingly. "And if you look closely, Bog's fourth eye is slightly greener."

"I'll remember that!" said Nelly. "You go and have fun. Be back by nine o'clock."

Just before nine o'clock, the
monsters arrived home with a napkin
full of mints.

"These are for you, Nelly. We've
been out for a meal and we've had a
lovely time."

"So have we, haven't we, girls!"
said Nelly.

Blotch and Bog gave Nelly a monster
hug and Nelly waved goodbye.

Chapter 4
A Monster Problem

The next day, Nelly had her own
phone plugged into her bedroom.

All the monsters in the
neighbourhood had heard about Nelly.

Nelly the monster-sitter was very
much in demand.

On Monday,
she sang
songs to
Curdle,
the prickly
baby monster
at Number 16.

On Tuesday, she played hide-and-seek with Gunk, the slimy little monster at Number 7.

On Wednesday, she did some colouring with Grimp, the half-hairy, half-feathery monster at Number 81.

On Thursday, she made muffins for Sludge, the slithery little monster at Number 38.

And on Friday, Nelly monster-sat the Squidlets at Number 2.

"I like being a monster-sitter," thought Nelly, happily.

It was Saturday evening at 5.45 when Nelly's phone rang again.

"Hello," said Nelly.

"Hello," said a faint and whispery voice. "Are you Nelly the monster-sitter?"

"That's me!" said Nelly.

"Could you please, please, please monster-sit for us this evening? We'd so, so, so like to go out and have some fun," croaked the voice.

"Of course I will. Where do you live?" said Nelly.

"Number 28," said the voice.

"I'll be round as soon as possible," said Nelly.

At 6.30, Nelly walked up the garden path of Number 28.

She pressed the doorbell. "I had no idea so many monsters lived in the street!" she smiled.

It was some minutes before Nelly heard footsteps shuffling towards the door.

The door handle turned and the door opened slowly. Two bloodshot eyes peered round the door at Nelly.

"Are you Nelly the monster-sitter?" said the voice.

"That's me!" smiled Nelly. "Can I come in?"

The door opened wide to reveal two stooping, drooping figures.

They had two arms, two legs and one head each, just like Nelly's mum and dad.

In fact they didn't look like monsters at all.

Slowly and wearily they turned and shuffled down the hallway.

"My name is Paul," whispered the man.

"My name is Caroline," groaned the woman.

Nelly followed them to the doorway of the living room, where Paul lifted his arm weakly and pointed.

"And this is Rowan."

Nelly stepped into the living room
and saw a little boy. He was standing on
the table with a play brick in his hand.

He looked at Nelly with wild eyes,
growled like a lion and threw the play
brick at her with a roar.

Nelly ducked as the play brick flew over her head and into the hallway.

"That's not all he does," groaned Paul. "He screams, shouts, bites, kicks, scratches and punches."

"The only thing he doesn't do," said Caroline, "is sleep."

"Mmmm," smiled Nelly. "You go and have a lovely time, I'll be fine with Rowan."

"Are you sure?" said Rowan's mum and dad.

"I'm sure," smiled Nelly. "Can you be back by nine o'clock?"

Nelly watched Rowan's mum and dad leave the house. When they had turned the corner at the end of the street, she closed the door.

She scratched her head for a moment and frowned. She had never babysat a monster like Rowan before.

She thought really hard. She scratched her head three more times.

Then she made a few phone calls on her mobile.

She was just sweeping up a vase that Rowan had thrown at the wall when the doorbell rang.

Nelly answered the door.

"Hullo, Hillooo, Hellope, Hollollolloo, Nelly," said the monsters. "How can we help?"

Chapter 5
Monsters to the Rescue

Nelly took the monsters into the living room to meet Rowan.

When Rowan saw them he picked up a toy car to throw at them.

"I can throw bigger things than you," said Freeb, picking up the armchair with one hand. "But I much prefer to do jigsaws."

Rowan put the toy car down
and growled.

"I can growl twice as loud as you," said
both of Lump's heads. "But I much prefer
to play with bricks."

Rowan stopped growling and made some gnashy noises with his teeth.

"I could bite the roof off this house if I wanted to," said Bog. "But I much prefer to do potato prints."

Rowan stopped gnashing and kicked out with his foot.

"We can kick, big time," said the Squidlets, lifting up their seven legs, "but we much prefer doing drawing."

Rowan stopped kicking and sat quietly down on the carpet.

Nelly smiled and went to get some gel pens.

At 8.30, Rowan's mum and dad returned home.

"These are for you," said Rowan's mum, handing Nelly a big packet of plasters and some bandages.

"I don't need those," said Nelly with a smile. "Have you had a lovely time?"

"We've had a lovely, lovely, lovely time. We went to the library and sat in wonderful, wonderful, wonderful peace and quiet."

"We've had a lovely, lovely, lovely time too," said Nelly, taking Paul and Caroline by the hand. She led them into the living room.

Paul and Caroline looked at Rowan in amazement. He was sitting on the carpet doing a jigsaw.

When he saw his mum and dad he jumped up, ran to them with a smile and gave them a great big kiss and a giant hug.

"Rowan!" said Caroline. "You're not a monster any more!"

"Nelly!" said Paul. "You're one in a million, you're a marvel, you're a star. You're the best monster-sitter in the world!"

Nelly smiled and blew them a monster kiss from the door.

"That's me!"

About the author

Is there a freckle on the back of your head?
Are there faeries at the bottom of your
garden? Are there gnomes living under your
carpet? Are there goblins in your sock drawer?
Are there monsters living in your street?

Just because you haven't seen them doesn't
mean that they're not there.